Welcome to ALADDIN QUIX!

If you are looking for fast, fun-to-read stories
with colorful characters, lots of kid-friendly
humor, easy-to-follow action, entertaining
story lines, and lively illustrations, then
ALADDIN QUIX is for you!

But wait, there's more!

If you're also looking for stories with
tables of contents; word lists; about-the-
book questions; 64, 80, or 96 pages; short
chapters; short paragraphs; and large fonts,
then **ALADDIN QUIX** is *definitely* for you!

ALADDIN QUIX: The next step between ready
to reads and longer, more challenging chapter
books, for readers five to eight years old.

Read all the books in the Royal Sweets series!

ROYAL SWEETS

Friends Forever

By Helen Perelman

Illustrated by Olivia Chin Mueller

ALADDIN QUIX

New York London Toronto Sydney New Delhi

For Heidi Klopfer, a royally good teacher and friend
—H. P.

ALADDIN QUIX
Simon & Schuster Children's Publishing Division
1230 Avenue of the Americas, New York, New York 10020
First Aladdin QUIX paperback edition May 2023
Text copyright © 2023 by Helen Perelman
Illustrations copyright © 2023 by Olivia Chin Mueller
Also available in an Aladdin QUIX hardcover edition.
All rights reserved, including the right of reproduction in whole or in part in any form.
ALADDIN and the related marks and colophon are trademarks of Simon & Schuster, Inc.
For information about special discounts for bulk purchases, please contact
Simon & Schuster Special Sales at 1-866-506-1949
or business@simonandschuster.com.
The Simon & Schuster Speakers Bureau can bring authors to your live event. For more information or to book an event contact the Simon & Schuster Speakers Bureau at 1-866-248-3049 or visit our website at www.simonspeakers.com.
Series designed by Jessica Handelman
Book designed by Tiara Iandiorio
The illustrations for this book were rendered digitally.
The text of this book was set in Archer Medium.
Manufactured in the United States of America 0323 OFF
2 4 6 8 10 9 7 5 3 1
Library of Congress Control Number 2022948894
ISBN 9781534476677 (hc)
ISBN 9781534476660 (pbk)
ISBN 9781534476684 (ebook)

Cast of Characters

Princess Mini: Royal fairy princess of Candy Kingdom

Queen Swirl and King Cone: Princess Mini's grandparents

Prince Scoop: Princess Mini's father

Butterscotch: Princess Mini's royal unicorn

Princess Lolli: Princess Mini's mother

Princess Cupcake and Prince Frosting: Princess Mini's cousins

Princess Taffy: Princess Mini's best friend

Spice: A Candy Narwhal

Lady Sherbet: Librarian at the Ice Cream Palace

Gobo: A troll living in Sugar Valley

Lady Dot and Duke of Syrup: Princess Taffy's parents from Sugar Kingdom

Contents

1

Sweet Cream Harbor

I, **Princess Mini**, love ice cream.

I have lots of ice cream when I visit my grandparents **Queen Swirl** and **King Cone** on Ice Cream Isles. My dad, **Prince Scoop**, is from there, and he knows all the

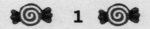

sweetest spots. Loving ice cream runs in my family!

Sometimes my parents have royal business at the Ice Cream Palace. During their meetings, I go exploring with **Butterscotch**, my unicorn. We always get back in time for an ice cream snack.

"You love ice cream too," I said to Butterscotch.

We were sitting on the sprinkle sands at Sweet Cream Harbor. The bright yellow sun was moving lower in the sky. My mother,

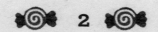

Princess Lolli, called this **"sun dip"** because the sun dropped behind the mountains.

The air smelled of sweet cream, and the sky was lavender with swirls of pink, orange, and blue. The wide harbor had milky white waters and big icy mountains all around. I watched Butterscotch as she licked the ice cream out of a large, round tub.

"I think vanilla chocolate chip is your favorite," I said.

Butterscotch swished her tail

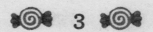

to the left and right. She lifted her head up, and her tongue wiped some ice cream on her **muzzle**. I giggled and scratched her ears. "Best part of the day, right?" I asked.

My parents were usually around for this late-afternoon ice cream snack. I looked back at the palace up on the hill. Their meeting must still be going on.

Today I was a little **impatient**. At breakfast my dad had promised to take me to see the ice

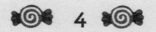

caves on the other side of the harbor. He told me that when he was a young Ice Cream Fairy, he went exploring there. I wondered why he wouldn't let me go alone. I was a first-year student at Royal Fairy Academy. Plus, Butterscotch would be with me.

I snapped my fingers and sprinkled more mini chocolate chips onto my ice cream. I had learned how to do that at Royal Fairy Academy. I held up my cone. **"Choc-o-rific!"** I exclaimed.

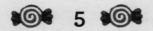 5

I finished my ice cream and licked my fingers. I dug my toes deep into the rainbow sprinkle sand. There were so many colors!

I wished that my friends were with me.

Even my cousins **Princess Cupcake** and **Prince Frosting** would have been good company. They bickered sometimes and were as opposite as sweet and sour, but I still would have liked to be with them. We were in the same class at school along with

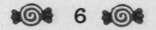

my best friend, **Princess Taffy**.

I looked out into the harbor.

"Just you and me," I said to Butterscotch.

Butterscotch rubbed her head on my arm. "I love you too," I told her.

The water was hitting the shore in a quiet and gentle rhythm.

Just then I saw something bobbing in the water.

What's that? I said to myself.

I squinted.

I stood up.

 7

I put my hand over my eyes to block out the setting sun.

Wait, was that a horn?

"Oh no!" I cried. "Butterscotch,

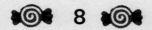

is that a unicorn in the harbor?"

I flapped my wings in worry.

Fairies and unicorns would be in trouble if their wings were wet! That would be a disaster.

I quickly flew down to the edge of the water with Butterscotch. Being a royal fairy princess, I wanted to help.

"Stay here," I told Butterscotch.

I didn't want her to go near the water. She couldn't risk getting wet.

When I got closer, I saw that

there was definitely a horn sticking out of the water.

But that was not a unicorn!

Who was this creature? I had to
find out!

2

Rainbow-tastic

"Hello!" I called out.

The small creature popped under the water.

"I didn't mean to scare you," I said. I took another step forward. "I would like to help you."

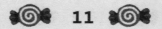

I waited.

Nothing happened.

Sure as sugar, I felt terrible. I didn't want to scare anyone.

"Please," I pleaded softly. "Are you okay?"

I waited. The milky water was still.

"I will not hurt you," I said. "I would like to help you."

The water rippled, and a shiny, twisted horn poked up. Two dark eyes stared back at me.

"Hello," I said. I leaned for-

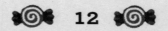 12

ward. "What is your name?"

"Hello," a small voice said. "I'm **Spice**." He pushed up and floated on top of the water.

"You are sugar-tastic!" I exclaimed.

Spice's horn was blue and sparkled in the sunlight. I didn't want to stare, but I couldn't help but **admire** his colors!

"Your horn is so sparkly!" I exclaimed.

Spice flipped his tail. "Thank you," he said. "Wait, who are you?"

"I am Princess Mini," I told him. "I am a royal Candy Fairy. I live in Candy Castle in Sugar Valley."

Spice nodded. "I have heard about Candy Fairies," he said. "Have you heard of Candy Narwhals?"

"My teacher Lady Cherry once read us a book about narwhals," I said. I could not take my eyes off Spice's sparkly horn. "I have never met one before."

"We are the unicorns of the sea," Spice said proudly.

I smiled at him.

"I went diving, and when I came back up, my **blessing** was gone," he said.

"Your blessing?" I asked.

"A blessing is a group of narwhals," Spice told me. He looked around.

"I was supposed to follow my mother," he said. "But I really wanted to see the sunken ship down there." He pointed his horn behind him. "I should have listened to my mother, but I wanted to explore."

I understood Spice's wanting to explore. "Your mother and the others were gone when you came back up?" I asked. "That is very scary."

"Yes," he said. "I need to find them."

He moved forward, and I saw that his back was spotted with a rainbow of colors.

"We passed by here last year, and I have been thinking about the ship," Spice told me. "I wanted to see inside it." He lowered his head. "Now I am not sure which way to go." He looked up at me. "Where am I?"

"You are in Sweet Cream Harbor," I said. "This is Ice Cream Isles." I pointed to the scoops of ice cream in the milky white harbor and then to the icy land behind me.

"I need to get to the North

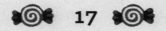

Sea," Spice told me. "Do you know which way I should go?"

I shook my head. "You said you were here last year," I said. "Do you remember anything else besides the sunken ship?"

"I remember large rainbow ice cones on the way," he said. "Just before the North Sea. Do you know where that would be?"

"Wait, what did those ice cones look like?" I asked.

Spice thought for a moment. "There were seven colorful swirls in the icy waters," he said. "Each one was a different color of the rainbow."

I shook my head. "I don't know where that is, but that sounds **rainbow-tastic**!" I exclaimed.

I remembered that there was

a large library in the Ice Cream Palace. My dad told me that he used to spend hours looking at all the books with maps.

"I think I can help you," I told Spice.

"Really?" he asked.

"I will be back," I said. "Stay nearby."

I hoped that I would find a book with the ice cones that Spice was describing.

And maybe I could help him find his family.

3

Ice Cone Cove

When I flew into the Ice Cream Palace, I saw that the meeting room door was closed. My parents were still in there.

I went down the long hall to the royal library.

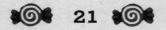 21

"Hello, Princess Mini," **Lady Sherbet** the librarian said.

Lady Sherbet had large orange wings, and she was wearing a pink dress with red, blue, and white sprinkles.

"Hello," I replied, flying up to her desk. "Do you have a book with maps?"

A smile spread across Lady Sherbet's face. "Here at the royal library, we have a whole area of books with maps," she said. She turned and pointed to four large bookcases.

"Thank you," I said. I flew over to the bookcases. There were more books of maps at the palace than I could have imagined!

I squinted up at all the books. I

wasn't sure where to start. Where were these ice cones that Spice saw?

"Are you looking for something?" Lady Sherbet asked. "Or someplace?"

I nodded. "Do you know about rainbow ice cones near here?" I asked her.

"Maybe in *Maps of Ice Cream Isles*," she said as she pulled a thick green book off the shelf. She put the book down on a table and flipped through the pages.

"**Ah!**" she exclaimed, pointing to one page. "This sounds like what you are describing. The place is called Ice Cone Cove!"

I leaned closer and saw a drawing of seven ice cones. Each cone was a different color of the rainbow. This was just what Spice had described! Up in the corner of the map, there was a symbol that looked like a **compass**. There was a large *N* with an arrow pointing to the North Sea.

"Are those rainbow ice cones close to the North Sea?" I asked.

Lady Sherbet smiled. "Yes, Princess Mini," she said.

I turned to the next page. There was a drawing of Candy Narwhals in the North Sea. I grinned—a blessing of narwhals in the North Sea! I had to let Spice know!

"How far is this from here?" I asked.

Lady Sherbet tapped her finger on her chin. "Too far for a Candy Fairy or a unicorn to fly," she said. "The North Sea is not near here."

My wings drooped. "May I

please take this book?" I asked. I
tried to use my best manners.

"Yes," Lady Sherbet said.
"Come back anytime!"

I put the book in my bag and flew out of the library. I couldn't wait to show Spice!

Stopping at a lake just past the drawbridge of the palace, I took a bucket and scooped up a few gummy fish. I wanted to bring Spice a sweet treat. I made sure to get all the flavors for him.

I was excited to tell Spice that I had found the ice cone clue.

But I did have a sinking feeling.

If the North Sea was too far to fly, how was I going to get there?

How could I help Spice if I couldn't
be there for him?

I needed some help.

As I flew to Sweet Cream Harbor,
I had a **sugar-tastic** idea.

I knew just who to call for help!

4

Sugar-tastic!

The sky was still full of color, even though the sun was almost past the **horizon**.

I wanted to deliver my news and the gummy fish to Spice before dark. I flew down to the part of the

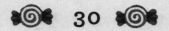

beach where the sweet cream hit the sprinkle sand.

Spice popped his head up and came closer to the shore. He moved around the ice cream scoops in the water.

"I have some gummy fish for you," I called.

"My favorite!" Spice answered. "Thank you!"

I threw the colorful fish to him in the water.

"I think I may have found a book that can help us," I told him.

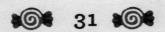 31

I held up the book so he could see. "It's a book of maps. On this map, there is Ice Cone Cove."

"**Yes!**" Spice said. "That's the place!"

I was glad to see his reaction. "The book also says that the narwhals return to the North Sea every year," I said. I turned to the next page and showed him the picture of Candy Narwhals in the sea. "And this shows that the North Sea is just above Ice Cone Cove."

Spice flipped his tail. I could tell he was happy.

"You can't fly, and I can't swim," I said. I sat down on a rock. "But don't worry, I have a

sugar-tastic idea!" I fluttered my wings and lifted off the rock.

Spice watched me. "What is your idea?" he asked.

"A boat!" I told him. "I can be in the water with you but not get my wings wet. You can swim along next to the boat, and you won't be alone. We can use the map, so we won't get lost."

"That is a supersweet idea!" Spice exclaimed. "Do you have a boat?"

I smiled. "My good friend has a

boat," I said. "I am going to send him a sugar fly message right now."

I called for a sugar fly to take a message to **Gobo**, a troll who lived in Chocolate Woods.

Spice watched the sugar fly take off. "I hope your friend can get here soon," he said.

"He will," I told Spice. "He won a boat race, and he knows the way here."

Spice swam closer to me. "You are a good friend, Princess Mini," he said.

I smiled. "I will be back tomorrow," I added. "Don't worry. **Help is on the way!**"

Spice's dark eyes looked down.

"Do you want to come back to the palace?" I asked.

Once I asked, I realized taking a Candy Narwhal to the palace wasn't the smartest idea. Where would he stay?

"I'm okay," he answered. "There is a school of fish here in the harbor. They have been nice to me."

"There's a school for fish?" I asked.

Spice laughed. "A group of fish is called a school!" he explained.

I laughed too. "You have taught me so much," I said.

I thought I saw Spice blush. "Thank you," he said.

"I will see you tomorrow," I called.

As I watched Spice swim away, I hoped Gobo and I would be able to sail to the North Sea quickly. Now more than ever, I wanted to be able to help Spice find his family.

5

Icy Surprises

The next morning I was flying in circles. My wings didn't stop moving. Did Gobo get my message? When would he get here?

At breakfast in the royal dining hall, Grandma Swirl scolded me.

"Mini, settle down," she said. "Your wings have not stopped fluttering!"

I sat down next to my mom at the long table. I tried to sit calmly like a good fairy princess.

"She's just excited for the day," Grandpa Cone said. He winked at me. I smiled and passed the sweet rolls across the table to him.

My dad flew into the dining room and handed me a sugar fly message. It was from Gobo! He was on his way!

"How long does it take to sail from Sugar Valley?" I asked my dad.

My dad sipped his fruit juice. "A few hours," he replied. "Is Gobo sailing up here?"

"Yes," I said. "Is that okay?"

"Yes," he answered. "I'm sorry we've been in meetings all day. I know I promised you a trip to see the ice caves."

I licked my sweet roll. "Maybe tomorrow?" I asked. I had big plans for today.

A palace guard flew into the room. "**Lady Dot** and **Duke of Syrup** from Sugar Kingdom have arrived," he **announced**.

I turned to the door. My best friend's parents were here! Could that mean that Taffy was here too?

"And Princess Taffy," the guard added.

I flew fast to hug her. I had never been so happy to see my friend!

"My parents came up for a meeting," Taffy said. "And they said I could come!"

"We thought this would be a fun surprise," my mom added. **"This is the sweetest surprise!"** I cried.

I looked at my parents and grandparents. They had worried looks on their faces. "What is happening in the kingdom?" I asked. I had a sour feeling about all these long meetings.

"There are more ice cubes in the North Sea than usual," my dad said. He sighed. "We are **concerned** about the oceans and the other small islands in the area."

I thought of Spice and his blessing. "What about the sea creatures and fish?" I asked.

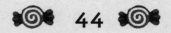

"They are fine," my mom said. "We are more concerned about the ice cubes blocking the area, and getting cones and ice cream to the rest of the kingdom."

"That is why we are here," Taffy's father said.

"Our syrup containers should be able to help with the extra ice," Lady Dot said.

"We hope," my dad whispered.

When our parents left the room, I told Taffy about Spice and getting him to the North Sea. I showed her the sugar fly message as well.

"Sweet!" Taffy said. Then she lowered her voice. "But what about the ice cubes?"

"I'm not sure," I said. "This is chilling news. We need to get to Spice."

Taffy and I flew to Sweet Cream Harbor. There was a cool breeze, and our wings fluttered in the wind.

I stood at the shoreline. I didn't see Spice. I was getting worried.

"Look!" Taffy said. "I see Gobo's boat!"

As the boat moved closer, I saw that there were other Candy Fairies on board. Frosting and Cupcake had come too. My cousins were here to help!

6

Ice Blocks

"Mini!" Frosting called, waving his arms.

Cupcake was holding on to the side of the boat. She didn't raise her hand to wave. I could tell she didn't really like being

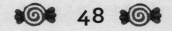

on Gobo's fast-moving boat.

Spice poked his head up from the water. "Hello," he said. He looked over at everyone with concern.

"This is my best friend, Princess Taffy," I said. "And on the boat are Gobo and Princess Cupcake and Prince Frosting. We are going to help you swim to the North Sea and find your family."

Gobo steered his boat up onto the beach.

"Hello!" he called.

"Meet Spice," I said, pointing at my new friend.

Spice spun around in the water, almost as if he were waving.

"Hot chocolate!" Frosting sang out. "It is really nice to meet you."

Frosting's eyes were wide. Seeing a Candy Narwhal was exciting.

Cupcake **peered** over the side of the boat.

"Sweet sprinkles!" she exclaimed.

Spice poked his sparkly horn

 50

up out of the water. I guess he was showing off a little!

I looked over at Cupcake. "Are you feeling okay?" I asked.

"Those were some huge waves," Cupcake said. She flew toward me and landed on the beach. "I am happy to be on land."

"We need to get moving," I said, grabbing her elbow. "We have to show Spice the way to the North Sea."

Taffy and I flew to the boat with Cupcake right behind us. I knew she didn't like sailing, but she also didn't want to miss out on an adventure.

Gobo sailed away from Sweet

Cream Harbor. "Here we go!" he cried.

"Thank you for coming," I said to Gobo. "You are a true friend and a lifesaver."

Gobo held on to the rope as he let the sail out to pick up speed. **"Happy to help!"** he said.

The wind swiftly carried us out to sea.

I watched Spice swim along-side Gobo's boat. My plan was working!

"There is Cone Island," Taffy

cried, pointing in front of the boat.

The island was full of sugar cones and wafer cones. **"Let's go back and visit!"**

Frosting exclaimed. He licked his lips. "I would love to spend some time there."

I checked the book of maps. "This means we are very close to Ice Cone Cove," I said.

"And the North Sea," Gobo said.

"Are we almost there?" Cupcake asked. She looked a funny shade of green.

I moved closer to Gobo. I wanted to tell him about the ice cubes.

But I was too late.

"Oh no!" Gobo shouted. He moved up front by the sailboat's **mast** to see ahead. "We're stuck!"

My wings were beating fast. My feet lifted off the boat. "Ice cubes?" I asked.

Gobo pointed in front of the boat. Large ice cubes were in the way.

"My parents were talking about all the ice cubes in the sea!" I exclaimed.

My wings dipped down low. I should have told Gobo sooner.

We had come so far, but we still had a long way to go.

7

Rainbow Bright

All around us there were large blocks of ice floating in the water. Gobo's boat couldn't move.

"I can't get past all these ice cubes," Gobo said.

"We're stuck!" Cupcake cried out.

"Hold on," I said. "Maybe Spice can help?"

Spice popped his head up. "I can use my horn," he said. He started chipping away at some of the ice and making a path for the boat.

"Good job!" Gobo cheered. He pulled on a rope, and the sail

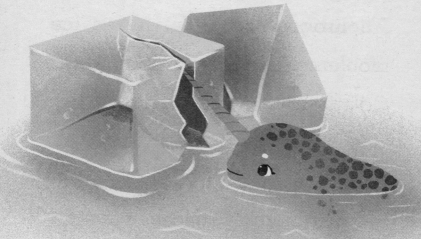

turned, filling up with air.

The boat sailed toward the North Sea.

Spice stayed ahead of the boat, working away at the ice.

"Maybe we could get the other narwhals to clear the North Sea," I said to Taffy. "This could be a **solution** to the North Sea ice problem!"

Taffy had a large grin on her face. "That is an **ice-tacular** idea!" she cheered.

Spice chopped the ice to make a

path for the boat, and Gobo sailed north. I think Spice knew he was close to his family as we passed Ice Cone Cove.

"Whoa!" Frosting said, looking at the seven large ice cones.

"Rainbow bright!" Cupcake said.

Taffy squinted. "I see something up ahead!" she exclaimed.

Frosting took out his binoculars. "Yes!" he cheered. "I see a few Candy Narwhals!"

"Hold on!" Gobo said. The wind

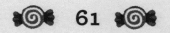

filled up the sail again, and we went speeding ahead.

I felt a strong gust of wind moving my wings. I grabbed hold of the boat.

I checked on Cupcake. She was gripping tightly onto the side of the boat.

The wind pushed our boat into the North Sea.

Frosting handed me his binoculars. Everything seemed so close when I looked through them.

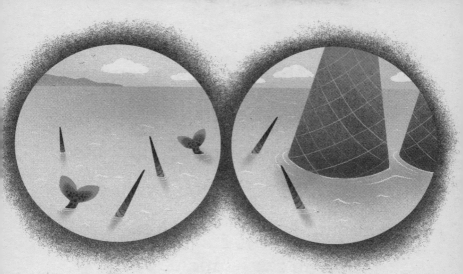

"You are right, Frosting!" I
exclaimed. "I see a few horns
sticking out of the water by that
large red ice cone."

"Sweet strawberries!"
Taffy cried. She pointed to the
circle of narwhals up head. They
were swimming to us.

"I think we found who we were looking for!" I cried.

Spice turned to face the boat. "I couldn't have done this without you," he said. "How can I ever thank you?"

I grinned. I was happy to help Spice and his family, and I knew exactly how he could help. "We do have a favor to ask," I said.

Spice and his blessing were happy to clear away the extra ice cubes that had formed in the cold waters. As they worked, I saw another boat approaching. High up on the tallest mast was a familiar flag. "Look!" I exclaimed.

My grandparents, my parents, and Taffy's parents were waving to us. They were on a large crystal syrup ship.

Taffy and I flew over to their boat. We explained how we had asked the narwhals to clear the ice.

Spice popped his head up next to their boat. "All clear!" he said. He tilted his head. "And thank you, Princess Mini!"

My parents hugged me. "This was your idea?" my mom asked.

"I had some help," I told her. I looked over at Gobo, Frosting, and Cupcake. "I have the best friends . . . and a special new friend."

Taffy and I flew back to Gobo's boat, and my friends and I watched Spice swim off. I was sorry to see my new friend leave. We all waved goodbye.

Spice turned and swam back to the boat.

"What's wrong?" I asked.

"I will pass this way next year," he said. "Will you be here?"

Spice's horn glittered in the

sun. I leaned down closer to the water.

"Sure as sugar," I told him.

I looked over my shoulder. I was lucky to have friends like them. I smiled at Spice. "You can count on us. We will be here. We are friends forever!"

Word List

admire (uhd•MY•ur): To think highly of

announced (uh•NOWNSD): Gave notice of arrival

blessing (BLEH•sing): A group of narwhals

compass (CUHM•puhs): A tool that shows the directions of north, south, east, and west

concerned (cuhn•SERND): Worried, troubled

horizon (huh•RY•zuhn): The line where the earth seems to meet the sky

impatient (im•PAY•shunt): Restless

mast (MAST): A long pole that sails can be attached to on a boat

muzzle (MUH•zuhl): The part of the horse's head that includes the mouth and nose

peered (PEERD): Looked curiously

solution (suh•LOO•shun): An answer to a problem

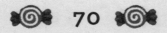

Questions

1. Where does Princess Mini first see Spice?

2. How did Spice get separated from his family?

3. What is the problem in the North Sea?

4. Who doesn't like being on Gobo's boat?

5. How does Spice help the Candy Fairies?

Fun Facts

- Narwhals live in the Arctic Ocean.
- Their "horns" (which are actually called "tusks") are spiral teeth growing up through their heads!
- A grown narwhal can be up to eighteen feet long.